PINKERTON, BEHAVE!
Steven Kellogg

 Dial Books for Young Readers an imprint of Penguin Group (USA) LLC

For HELEN,
my best friend
and the person
who chose
the Great
Pinkerton

Lick Lick Lick Lick Lick Lick Lick Lick Lick Lick Lick Lick Lick Lick Lick Lick Lick Lick Lick Lick Lick Lick Lick Lick Lick Lick Lick Lick Lick Lick Lick Lick Lick Lick Lick Lick Lick Lick Lick Lick Lick Lick Lick Lick Lick Lick Lick Lick

Photographs by Tom Crider

A note from Steven Kellogg

In this thirty-fifth anniversary edition of *Pinkerton, Behave!* the oversized firearm that was originally included as part of the burglar's stereotyped caricature has been reconsidered and eliminated. This revision in the text and illustrations provided the opportunity to make other adjustments designed to heighten the celebration of the irrepressible Great Dane puppy who brought merriment and chaos into our family during the decade following his arrival in 1976.

DIAL BOOKS FOR YOUNG READERS

Published by the Penguin Group · Penguin Group (USA) LLC
375 Hudson Street · New York, New York 10014

USA / Canada / UK / Ireland / Australia / New Zealand / India / South Africa / China

penguin.com
A Penguin Random House Company

Library of Congress Cataloging-in-Publication Data · Kellogg, Steven, author, illustrator. · Pinkerton, behave! / Steven Kellogg.
pages cm · Originally published in 1979. · Summary: "Pinkerton may not be the best-trained dog in his class, but his unconventional behavior saves the day when a burglar comes to his house"— Provided by publisher. · ISBN 978-0-8037-4130-0 (hardcover) · [1. Dogs—Training—Fiction. 2. Behavior—Fiction.] I. Title. · PZ7.K292Pi 2014 · [E]—dc23 · 2013044869 · Manufactured in China on acid-free paper

1 3 5 7 9 10 8 6 4 2

Text set in Cosmiqua Com

The full-color artwork was prepared using ink and pencil line, watercolor washes, and acrylic paints.

Every new puppy has to learn to behave.

First I'll teach Pinkerton to come when he's called.

While he's trying to master COME, we'll teach him to FETCH my slippers.

From now on I'll fetch my own slippers.

But it's important for him to defend the house if a burglar shows up.
He'll need to BARK LOUDLY to scare the bad guy away.

I'm afraid Pinkerton needs professional help.

He'll have to go to obedience school.

When this poor creature sees how well my other pupils behave, he will understand what I expect of him.

We begin with the simple command.

We cannot hold back the entire class for one confused student.
ON TO THE NEXT LESSON!

Your dog's misbehavior sets a poor example for the other students.
Unless he shows immediate improvement, he will be dismissed!

We will now review all that we have learned.
Begin with the simple command.

Mom, you've had a pretty rough day. Why don't you go to bed and get a good night's sleep?

Pleasant dreams, Mom. Pleasant dreams, Pinkerton.

Pinkerton, wake up! It's a bad guy! Scare him away!

Pinkerton, he's a slipper!

Pinkerton, I'm a bad guy.

We love you, Pinkerton.